My Granny
Is A Sumo Wrestler

Gareth Owen

Young Lions

More Young Lions poetry

The Song that Sings the Bird *ed. Ruth Craft*
Come on into my Tropical Garden *Grace Nichols*
Toughie Toffee *ed. David Orme*
Salford Road *Gareth Owen*
Song of the City *Gareth Owen*
Mind Your Own Business *Michael Rosen*
Hairy Tales and Nursery Crimes *Michael Rosen*
Out of the Blue *ed. Fiona Waters*
The Lions Book of Young Verse *ed Julia Watson*
A Children's Zoo *ed. Julia Watson*
Rabbiting On *Kit Wright*

MY GRANNY IS A SUMO WRESTLER

Gareth Owen

Illustrated by John Bendall-Brunello

Young Lions
An imprint of HarperCollinsPublishers

For John Hemming

First published in Great Britain in Young Lions 1994

Young Lions is an imprint of HarperCollins Children's Books, a division of
HarperCollins Publishers Ltd, 77-85 Fulham Palace Road,
Hammersmith London W6 8JB
1 3 5 7 9 10 8 6 4 2

ISBN 0 00 674883 X

Printed and bound in Great Britian by HarperCollins
Manufacturing Ltd, Glasgow

Contents

My Granny is a Sumo Wrestler   7

The Artist   9

New Boy   10

Genes   12

Empty House   13

The Boyhood of Dracula   14

Moon   16

Talking to Trees   17

Death of a Ghost   18

Why Did You Call Me Percy?   24

Mazurkatee   26

Ambitions   28

My Bed's a Silver Spaceship   29

Universal Zoo   31

Today We're Going to Write a Poem!   32

Paper Wrap   33

Midnight Snow   39

The Human Exhibition   41

Nightmare   44

In a Pickle   45

The Midnight Mail   46

Kite   48

Life as a Sheep   49

Funny Man   51

Reflections   53
Cousin Janice With the Big Voice   55
Star Gazing   56
Launderette   58
The Secret   59
School Outing   62
Postbox   64
Rosie McAluskey   65
The Hedgehog   67
A Young Girl Came Riding   68
Badger   70
Before the Beginning   71
Rubble   72
Basil   75
Bedmobile   76
A Poem For a Very Special Person   77
Pearl   80
Eat It All Up   81
There and Back Again   83
Turkey and Pig   84
Scatterbrain   87

My Granny Is A Sumo Wrestler

My granny is six foot three
My granny is built like a tree
My granny says - **Nothing**
I mean nothing
Frightens me.

When Granny walks down the streets
She scares every man she meets
Nobody gonna mess with her
My granny is a Sumo Wrestler.

My granny is six foot three
My granny she's built like a tree
My granny says - **Nothing**
I mean nothing
Frightens me.

My granny does what she likes
My granny rides two motor bikes (at the same time)
My granny she breaks down doors
My granny bends bars with her jaws.

My granny she's six foot three (that's sitting down)
My granny she's built like a tree
My granny says - **Nothing**
Absolutely nothing
Frightens me.

My granny is a railway ganger
My granny is a wild head banger
My granny eats uncooked bison
My granny beat up Mike Tyson (in the first round).

My granny she's six foot three
My granny she's built like a tree (oak tree)
My granny says - **Nothing**
And I mean nothing
Ever
      Ever
           EVER
                Frightens me.

The Artist

I painted a brilliant picture
The greatest ever seen
It hung in the National Gallery
And was purchased by the Queen.
This most wonderful of paintings
Is called 'Polar Bears in the Snow'
And in case you don't believe me
I've included it below.

New Boy

He stood alone in the playground
Scuffed his shoes and stared at the ground
He'd come halfway through term from the Catholic
　　school
On the other side of town.

He'd a brand new blazer and cap on
Polished shoes and neatly cut hair
Blew on his fists, looked up and half-smiled
Pretending he didn't care.

And I remembered when I'd be new
And no one had spoken to me
I'd almost cried as I stood alone
Hiding my misery.

Heart said I should go over,
Share a joke or play the fool
But I was scared of looking stupid
In front of the rest of the school.

At break someone said they'd seen him
Crying in the geography test
And when he came out they pointed and laughed
And I laughed along with the rest.

In my dreams I'd always stood alone
Believing I was the best
But in the cold playground of everyday life
I was no better than the rest.

Genes

They say I've got my father's nose
They say I've got his walk
And there's something about my grandad
In the serious way I talk.

'And aren't his legs just like our Jack's?'
Says smiling Auntie Rose
'*He* could bend over just like that
And touch his head with his toes.'

I've got Auntie Julia's funny laugh
I've sister Betty's lips
And just like Sid on my mother's side
I'm fond of fish and chips.

I have moods that remind them of Auntie Vi
And my hair's just like their Paul
When I look at myself in the mirror at home
I wonder if I'm me at all.

But what I ask myself is this –
Why does it have to be
Me who looks like them and not
Them who look like me?

Empty House

I hate our house when there's no one in
I miss my family and I miss the din.
The rooms and the hallway seem cold and bare
And the silence hangs like dust in the air.
What's that sound upstairs that makes me start
Driving Fear like an icicle through my heart?
I'm imagining things, there's nobody there –
But I have to make sure so I creep up the stair
I stand holding my breath by the bedroom door
And hear something rustling across the floor.
Then a scratching sound, a tiny cry!
I can't seem to breathe, my throat is dry.
In the silence I hear my own heart beating
And the rumble of water in the central heating.
I should go in but I just don't dare
So I call aloud, 'Is anyone there?'
Nobody answers. I push open the door
A fluttering shadow crosses the floor.
And now I see him, now understand
And I gather him gently in my hands.
'I won't hurt you, my friend. Don't flutter, don't start.'
But his body beats wild like a feathered heart.
Out through the window, watch him wheel and fly
Carrying my fear across the sky.

The Boyhood of Dracula

So we let him join us
In the game of Hide and Seek
Because Joanna said we ought,
She being the biggest of us all
And bossy with it.
And him standing there
All hunched and trembling
In the thin snow by the stable door
Watching us like some poor lost soul
With those great eyes he had.
Well, you'd be a thing of stone
To take no pity on the boy.
You never saw a soul
So pale and woebegone;
His pinched nose raw with cold
And naught to keep the bitter wind
The right side of his bones
But that old bit of musty cloak
He always seems to wear.

Poor little mite
You'd think, to watch,
He'd never played the game before.
Maureen Cantelow,
The parson's youngest girl
From Norton Campion way,
She found him straight away
Hardly bothering to hide at all
Among the meal sacks
In the lower barn.

Poor girl,
She must have cut herself
In there somehow
For as I spied them
Running hand in hand below
She sowed fresh seeds of crimson blood
Across ridged and bitter snow.

Moon

'The moon is thousands of miles away,'
My Uncle Trevor said.
Why can't he see
It's caught in a tree
Above our onion bed?

Talking to Trees

Grandad talks to trees
You can hear him nattering
When the garden's empty.
'Hello, Oak,' he says,
'How do, Willow?
How's tricks this morning, Ash?'
Then he moves on down
To the fruit and veg
Like a general
Inspecting a line of troops.
'Well now, Rhubarb,
You've come on a bundle
Since I saw you last.
How's my old mate Sprout?'

Mum was embarrassed
In case the neighbours heard.
And dad asked
Laughing up his sleeve,
'Don't they ever answer back?'
''Course they don't,'
Said Grandad.
'That's the whole point.
What d'you think they are?
People?'

Death of a Ghost

Now none of us had ever
Actually seen the ghost,
Though some – like Raymond Pudsey
And his mate – would boast
They'd once stayed out all night
And seen this knight, striding
At midnight past the ditch
Where they were hiding.
'Course, none of us believed
A word of it. *I* knew –
We *all* knew – Raymond Pudsey
Never spoke a true
Word in his life. But then
All of us believed the tales
Of the ghostly knight who
Roamed the hills and dales
Searching for the bitter foe
Who'd stabbed him one dark night
Nine hundred years ago.

They said the wounds from which
The knight had died
Still dripped fresh blood
That never, ever dried.
Many's the night I lay
In bed and couldn't sleep
Imagining I heard his footsteps
Climbing up the steep,
Rough pathway to our house.
My grandma'd threaten me
If I should misbehave with,
'Sure as sure one day
He'll rise up from the grave
And carry you away.'
'Don't you believe a word
She says,' my dad would say.
But even now sometimes
I wake up in the night
And think he's out there waiting,
Somewhere beyond the light.

Did anybody see it?
Colley's grandad did,
When rolling home one night
From Weston Dale so dead
With drink he slipped and fell
Into a field of corn –
This was long before
You or me was born.
He staggered to his feet again
And stumbled cursing
Through this sea of grain
Until he found himself
Staggering down the Fosse
Up on the hilltop where
The four lanes cross.
He stops. Hears a sound
And turning, sees this shadow
Rising from the ground.
'Course, first of all he thinks
What anyone would think:
Here's another bound for home
Something the worse for drink.
So Colley's grandad cries aloud,

'Who's there? Give me your aid!'
And not a word the stranger says
But three times waves a shimmering blade
Above his head, and striding past
Seems to vanish into air
Leaving the sound of battle
Still raging everywhere.

What was it like?
Its face was pale. It wore
A sort of chain mail hood
Which Colley's grandad swore
Was dyed deep red with rust
Or maybe it was blood.
Its eyes were closed,
The mouth a gaping wound
Screaming for revenge
But yet it made no sound.
As it passsed it seemed
To do its best to strike
At Colley's grandad with
A kind of lance or pike.
And that was all.

Old Colley ran,
His feet scarce touched the ground
Until he shut the door
Behind him, safe and sound.
Shaking with fright, he fell
Into his bed and wept
With fear at what he'd seen
Till finally he slept.

The sun shone bright, the birds
Sang sweet the following day.
The apparition seemed
A million miles away.
Old Colley laughed and told his wife
What drink had made him see,
But she turned pale as gin
And pointed trembling
To where her husband stood.

The white shirt that he wore
Ran red with crimson blood.
No matter how they tried
The blood flowed swift and fresh
Although no wound nor mark
Had scarred his flesh.

Well, that's our village legend
I've nothing more to say –
Except for something strange
That happened just the other day.
An Oxford archaeologist
Began to dig the ground
Where folk there reckoned
The knight would likeliest be found.
For three long weeks he dug
While we all watched, our faces grim
Whispering to each other,
'What has *our* ghost to do with him?'

Then, one cold and rainy morning
Six feet beneath the ground
The man unearthed a coffin
And inside it found
Remains. The whole village
Stared in deep dismay
As our poor ghost was dragged into
The clear light of day;
A tiny pile of mouldering bones,
Broken wood and rust
And in the steady falling rain
A legend slowly turning into dust.

Why Did You Call Me Percy?

Dad,why did you call me Percy?
Why did you give me that name?
I only have to think of it
And I go puce with shame.
Mum,why did you call me Percy?
It's a name that no one would want
Did you suffer some kind of brainstorm
When you named me at the font?
What was wrong with David
Or Fred or Wayne or Sam
Or any other kind of name
That sounds like what I am?
Percy sounds like someone
Who helps his mother cook
Brings apples for the teacher
Presses wild flowers in a book.
Who goes skipping through the countryside
Or keeps a budgie for a pet
Who cries when soap gets in his eyes
Or when his feet get wet.
I'd love to be something like Conan
Or someone with a name like Keith

Who sings and dances on the stage
And plays guitars with his teeth.
And what was wrong with Eddie
Or Rod or Cliff or Rick
Or Jimmy, Ben or Phil or Geoff
Or Elvis, John or Mick?
But Percy, stupid Percy
It goes through me like a knife
Did you never think when you called me that
He'd be with me all my life?

Mazurkatee

Mazurkatee the brindled cat
Leapt smiling from the ark
And hitched a lift to Humansville
Where he thought he'd have a lark.
He jumped aboard a pick-up truck
That drove him into town
And flashed his smile at all he met
While sauntering up and down.
The lady at the check-out till
Was straightening up her seams
Applying rouge to both her cheeks
And adding up her dreams.

Beneath the portals of the bank
A rich man knelt and prayed
To a statue dedicated
To the money he had made.
And on the ancient shores of Time
A ragged beggar sat
His pockets full of emptiness
And raindrops in his hat.
And the cat they called Mazurkatee
Could read the hearts of men
And all that he found written there
He multiplied by ten.
And when he'd learned what all men know

He stored it in his brain
Then sat forever in a tree
And never smiled again.

Ambitions

'When you grow up what will you be?'
I opened my dictionary at random to see
And stabbed with my finger,
'That's what I'll be.
Has anyone heard of lycanthropy?'

My Bed's a Silver Spaceship

When I wake up some mornings
Not all is what it seems
I drift in a land of make-believe
Between my real life and my dreams.

Strange creatures from the stories
That I read the night before
Crowd in upon my drowsiness
Through imagination's door.

Where sleep and waking overlap
The alarm clock's jangling cry
Is a roaring fire-tailed rocket
Hurtling through the sky.

My bed's a silver spaceship
Which I pilot all alone
Whispering through endless stratospheres
Towards planets still unknown.

Outside through morning mistiness
The spinning lights of cars
In my make-believe space voyage
Become eternities of stars.

Is that mother calling something
My dreams can't understand?
Or can it be crackling instructions
From far-off Mission Command?

If I make believe my ceiling
Is space through which I fly
If I make believe my bedroom
Is my capsule flying high
If I make believe the lightbulb
Is a planet passing by
If I make believe my blanket
Is its cratered surface dry
Then that's what it is for me
Yes, that's what it is
That's what it is
That's what it is for me.

Universal Zoo

The creatures of the world one day
Packed sandwiches and tea
And toured the Universal Zoo
To see what they could see.

And all alone in a tiny cage
Sat a child on an unmade bed
With the words 'Endangered Species' scrawled
On the wall above his head.

Today We're Going to Write a Poem!

I close my eyes and try to drift
Into a world of poetry thoughts.
You know the kind of thing they like:
Clouds and snow and nodding daffodils.
But then I see my Uncle Glynn at Grendon Green
Whistling in his herd of cows.
They trundle though the muck into the shed
Their heavy udders swaying
Veined, and full of milk.
Then suddenly my mum is there
Selling these moccasins
That she makes at home
To sell at Ledbury Market.
The paper bag is twirled till it has ears.
She flings a shower of coins into the till.
I shake my head. This won't do.
You can't write poems about moccasins
Udders, money, muck and tills.
I push my mind back to poetic thoughts:
Clouds, banks of snow and dancing daffodils.

Paper Wrap

This is me on a roll
At the back of a shop
Only wrapping paper
But I'm full of hip-hop.

Wanna wrap a kettle
Wanna wrap a china cup
Tear me off a stripperoo
And watch me wrap them up.

'Cos I'm wrapping paper
Wrap anything you see
But no one gives a monkey's
When they're all through with me.

They take me to their houses
And, isn't this a sin?
They rip me all to pieces
And chuck me in a bin.

And me, I'm getting tired
I'm a roll of misery
Dream of breaking out of here
Dream of being free.

So one rainy evening
When I'd really had enough
Made my mind up there and then
I was going to cut up rough.

Waited in the darkness
Until they closed the shop
Then started to unroll myself
I just wouldn't stop.

Heard the watchman singing
His finger on his gun
Jumped him down by Fancy Goods
His singing days were done.

He didn't know what hit him
Didn't even shout
When wrapping paper's on the loose
You'd better all look out.

I snaked across the counter
And stole across the floor
Heard the city calling me
And smashed out through the door.

The patrolman shone his flashlight
Radioed back to base
'There's something weird near Harrods'
And it doesn't have a face!'

The policeman gasped with terror
'Is this a joke?' he muttered
They were the final words, my friends
That flatfoot ever uttered.

A cleaner in the sewer
Working far below
No one heard his dying cry,
'It's the Wrapper! **No!** Oh *Noooooooooooooo!*

Rolling through the midnight streets
Wrap anyone I see
Schoolgirls, priests or criminals
All come the same to me.

There's a pair of late-night lovers
Five revellers in the rain
A drunken man who'll never see
His home, sweet home, again.

And it's – Look out! Here's the bogeyman
Better close your doors
The next house that I visit
Could be yours or yours or yours.

If you peep out through your curtains
That's my shadow on the sky
So hide your eyes my darlings
When the Wrapper's rolling by.

And little children everywhere
Don't ask your mummies why
Just close your eyes my darlings
When I come rolling by.

And it's – **NIGHTMARE ON WRAP STREET!**
It's headlines in the paper
It's – **ENTIRE CITY EATEN ALIVE
    BY PSYCHO WRAPPING PAPER.**

The minister chews his fingernails
There are questions in the press
Vera Lynn is singing songs
To the troops and the SAS.

It's – **'Batman, do you read me?
Please save us if you can.'**
It's – **'Call the good ship Enterprise'**
It's – **'Send for Superman.'**

But me, I'm right behind you
As the night begins to lift
Wrapping up the BBC
Like a pretty Christmas gift.

10 Downing Street and Oxford Street
St Paul's, The Albert Hall,
Just throw myself around them
Wrap one, wrap two, wrap all.

Wrapped up Heathrow Airport
And Concorde flying over
Wrapped up tight the Sussex Downs
And the white cliffs of Dover.

Rolled myself down Wembley Way
Wrapped up all the players
Rolled across to Kathmandu
There go the Himalayas.

And now the round and turning world
Was gift-wrapped tight and neat
There was nothing left for me to do
My life's work was complete.

Felt a touch of emptiness
Turned back to my old shelf
There was nothing left to wrap around
So I wrapped around ...

Midnight Snow

One night as I lay sleeping
And dreams ran through my head
The night breeze stirred my curtain
And moonlight bathed my bed.
I walked up to the window
And leaned upon the ledge
Saw drifting snowflakes falling
On road and lane and hedge.

Midnight snow
Drifting slow
While the world lies sleeping
And only me, here to see
Those snowflakes gently falling.

And all along the roadway
The blanket lies unstirred
No tracks of tyres or sledges
No print of fox or bird.
No footsteps in the garden
No sound upon the air
A million petals falling
Silent as a prayer.

Midnight snow
Drifting slow
While the world lies sleeping
And only me, here to see
Those snowflakes gently falling.

Taken from the Welsh hymn:
Y Milwr Bychan by Joseph Parry

The Human Exhibition

In the Museum of Mankind
Mum gave me this look
When I said so loud
That everyone could hear,
    'I want to go to the toilet.'
Dad looked at his watch.
'We'll meet you by Human Growth
In five minutes from now.'
As I walked away I heard
Uncle Peter say to Auntie Lill,
'Let's visit the dinosaurs
And meet some of your relations.'

When I came out
I couldn't see them anywhere
And ran into a room called
Life Before Birth.
All of sudden the lights went out
And a robot voice whispered,
    'This is your mother!'
A gigantic ten foot baby
Lit from inside
Hung pink and hovering in the air
Its heartbeat thundering out.
It was a relief to see dad's bald head at last
Gleaming beneath a Human Ageing sign.

But when I tapped him on the back
He had the wrong face on.
     'Sorry, sorry,' I said
And ran towards the entrance
Searching the faces
For someone that I knew
But all the world was strangers.
Lost, I thought. I'm lost
And though I didn't want them to
Hot tears came in my eyes.
I ran back to Life Before Birth
But my mum was nowhere.

An old lady in a floor-length kilt
Offered me her lacy hanky
To wipe away my tears
Then passed me on to this attendant.
He led me through
Lost Tribes of the Amazon Rainforest.
     'Anyone here you know?' he asked.
I shook my head.
When a boy with green hair
And a skull and crossbones on his jacket
     Said, **'Look, that kid's crying!'**
I pretended I had something in my eye.

Then looking round I saw my Uncle Peter
Pretending he was playing the xylophone
On the pterodactyl's tail
And Auntie Lill crimson round the neck
Pretending she was on her own.
Mum squealed and hugged me till I squeaked
Then told me off for half an hour
Then cried and hugged me once again.

We went to the café for tea
And Uncle Peter bought me
An Angelica doughnut with cherries on the top.
I looked round.
All those people!
Feeding their faces fit to bust,
Slurping tea and fizzy drinks
Cheeks munching and bulging
Bulging and munching.
The Human Exhibition.

Nightmare

Someone came walking through my dreams
Across a lake of blood
And though I turned to run, my feet
Were rooted where they stood.

Within the prison of my dream
I struggled to break free
But nearer and nearer the figure came
Across the lake to me.

The hollow sockets of his eyes
Held me in his glare
And though I raised my voice to scream
My voice was soundless air.

At last I woke but still my heart
Beat with an awful dread
For there the sightless figure stood
Smiling beside my bed.

In a Pickle

Antoinette Pickles
Never moved far
Lived with pickled onions
In a pickled-onion jar.
Onions on her right side
Onions on the other
Onions at her head and heels
All bottled by her mother.

Her friends who came to visit her
Were all distinctly tickled
To read the label on the jar,
'Here's Antoinette, quite pickled.'

The Midnight Mail

Have you ever woken up
In the middle of the night?
Have you ever woken up
In an awful fright?

Have you woken from a dream
With a dreadful start?
And heard a drum beating
A tattoo in your heart?

And the night is as black
As a witch's hat
And you think to yourself
What was that? What was that?

What was that? What was that?
Made the windows shake
Made the saucepans rattle
And the whole house quake?

What was that? What was that?
It's the Midnight Mail
Thundering past my bedroom.
On its iron rail.

Now further off and further off,
Out of earshot, out of sight
Swifter than an arrow
Hurtling through the night.

Now quieter and more quiet
Till a still silence falls
On trees and roads and houses
And moss-covered walls.

And I think about the Midnight Mail
Thundering on her way
Waking someone in a bedroom
A hundred miles away.

Kite

On Parbold Hill my red kite swirled
Caught in the same high draught that whirled
The crows and set the grey torn shreds
Of cloudlets streaming overhead.
It tugged my fist insistently
Like something longing to be free
Of earth. And oh, I dreamed we two
Soared on the air as wild birds do
Breasting the west wind, ever higher
Over the fields of Lancashire
Out of the clouds, into the light
Smaller now and gaining height
Until at long last out of sight.

Life as a Sheep

Sometimes
Oi stands
Sometimes
Oi sits
Then
Stands again
Then
Sits
For a bit.

Sometimes
Oi wanders
Sometimes
Oi stays
Sometimes
Oi chews
Sometimes
Oi strays.

Sometimes
Oi coughs
Sometimes
Oi don't
Sometimes
Oi bleats
Sometimes

Oi won't.
Sometimes
Oi watch
The human race
Or
Smiles to meself
Or
Stares into space.

And when
Oi's happy
Oi'd dance and sing
But Oi
Don't have the knack
To do
Such a thing.

At night
Oi lays
By the old church steeple
And
Falls asleep
By counting people.

Funny Man

There's a funny bloke called Albert
Lives at Number Twenty-Five
Plays a silver cornet with his ear
Keeps piglets in a hive.

He dances on his ownsome
By the lightsome brightsome stars
And keeps giant snails in metal pails
And his teeth in pickle jars.

He bathes starkers in a barrel
Beneath a hornbeam tree
And hides his head inside a sack
In case anyone should see.

He mows his bathroom carpet
And hoovers all the grass
Sings cadenzas to the sparrows
As they flitter-flutter past.

Wears a suit of rusty armour
Whenever he's in bed
And a green and yellow cosy
To warm his old, bald head.

But you'd best not laugh at Albert
You'd best not mock, my dears
For Albert could be you, d'you see
In sixty-five short years.

Reflections

Reflections

Here we are
At the mirror
Again
Me and him
Him and me
Staring and changing
Changing and staring.
Every single day
It's like this;
That hair
Those eyes
That nose.
And he
That other one there
Know what he does?
Gives me that smile
That sincere smile
The one he tries on me each day.
And me? I smile straight back.
He doesn't fool me
Not for a minute
That smile may work on others
Not on me.
I tell him straight
No messing.
I say – 'Listen you,

Whoever you are,
I can see through you
See through that smile.
You want to be careful.
I know what you're about
Better watch your step
Or with a tiny breath
I'll wipe you out.'

Whoever you are,
I can see through you
See through that smile.
You want to be careful.
I know what you're about
Better watch your step
Or with a tiny breath
I'll wipe you out.'

Cousin Janice with the Big Voice

When my cousin Janice
Opens her mouth to speak
A storm kindles behind her teeth
And a gale pours out.
This is a voice used
To holding conversations
With cows and sheep and dogs
Across mountains and valleys
But here across the tablecloth
In our small flat
When she asks for the sugar
The teacups tremble
And a tidal wave foments
In the eddies of the cherry trifle.

Star Gazing

At midnight through my window
I spy with wondering eye
The far-off stars and planets
Sprinkled on the sky.

There the constant North Star
Hangs above our trees
And there the Plough and Sirius
And the distant Pleiades.

Star on star past counting
Each one a raging sun
And the sky one endless suburb
With all her lights left on.

How strange it is that certain stars
Whose distant lights still glow
Vanished in that sea of space
Three million years ago.

And if I stare too long a time
The stars swim in my eyes
Drifting towards my bedroom
Down the vast slopes of the sky.

And, mesmerised, I wonder,
Will *our* Earth someday die?
Spreading her fabric and her dreams
In fragments on the sky.

And then my imagination
Sees in some distant dawn
A young girl staring skywards
On a planet still unborn.

And will she also wonder,
Was there ever life out there?
Before the whole thing vanished
Like a dream into the air.

Launderette

Wishy, washy, there's my shirt
Swirling squirming round my vest.
Splashy, dashy, two red socks
In a sandwich with the rest.
A football scarf, a bright-red hat
A pillow-slip, blue jeans, a sheet.
Oh, my goodness, what was that?
A hand, a face, a pair of feet
Someone swirling round quite bare –
How did Granny get in there?

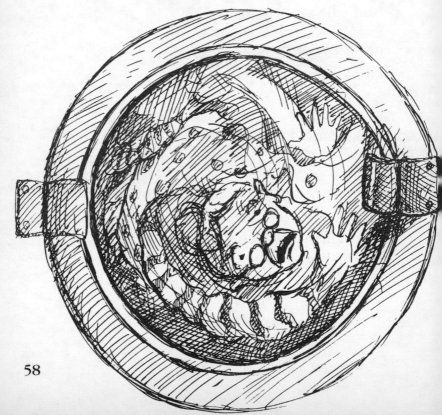

The Secret

Down a secret path
Through a secret wood
By the shore of a secret sea
I creep on tiptoe
To a place that I know
That no one has seen except me
Except me
That no one has seen except me.

And the soft wind that blows
Through the briar and the rose
That I pass along the way
Seems to whisper low,
Nobody must know
The secret you've learned today
Today
The secret you've learned today.

Down by a beach
Where the herring gulls screech
And the long white breakers roll
The voice of the sea
Whispers softly to me,
You must not tell a soul
A soul
You must not tell a soul.

But my secret somehow
Seems to grow and grow
Till it weighs me down like a load
Oh, I must tell someone
Before very long
Or I think I'm going to explode
Explode
Or I think I'm going to explode.

I climb up from the beach
Till I finally reach
A valley, deep and wide
And it's there that I tell
To an old stone well
The secret I carry inside
Inside
The secret I carry inside.

In that well's stone ear
Where no one can hear
I whisper secretly
And from far away
Each word I say
Comes echoing back to me
To me
Comes echoing back to me.

And I make that well
Promise never to tell
What I've whispered so secretly
Then clear as a bell
Speaks the voice of the well,
'Your secret is safe with me
With me
Your secret is safe with me.'

School Outing

Class Four, isn't this wonderful?
Gaze from your windows, do.
Aren't those beauteous mountains heavenly?
Jut drink in that gorgeous view.

Sir, Linda Frost has fainted
Aw Sir, I think she's dead
And Kenny Mound's throwing sandwiches round
I've got ketchup all over my head.

Oh, aren't these costumes just super?
Please notice the duchess's hat!
You can write up your notes for homework tonight,
I know you'll look forward to that.

Sir, Antoinette Toast says she's seen the ghost
Of that woman, Lady Jane Grey
And I don't know where Billy Beefcake is
But the armour is walking away.

And here in this ghastly dungeon
The prisoners were left to die
Oh, it's all just so terribly touching
I'm afraid I'm going to cry.

Sir, Stanley Slack has put Fred on the rack
Sir, somebody's pinched my coat
Sir, Melanie Moreland's dived off the wall and
Is doing the crawl round the moat.

Well, here we are, homeward bound again –
It's been a wonderful day
I know when you meet your parents and friends
You'll have so many things to say.

Sir, what is that siren wailing for?
Sir, what's that road block ahead?
Sir, Tommy Treat is under the seat
Wearing a crown on his head.

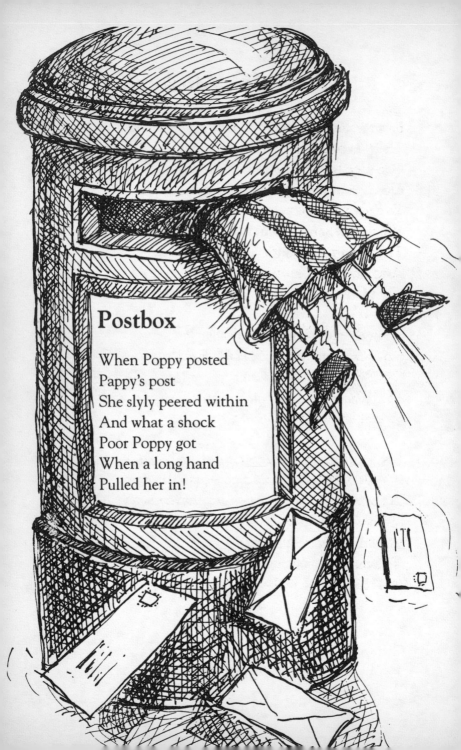

Postbox

When Poppy posted
Pappy's post
She slyly peered within
And what a shock
Poor Poppy got
When a long hand
Pulled her in!

Rosie McAluskey

From a standing start
The two of us
Can race the leccy train
Out of Ainsdale Station
To the first telegraph pole
Where the sandhills begin.
The live line crackles
And smells of lightning.
'One foot on that
And you're nowt
But a pile of smoking ash,'
Rosie tells me smiling.
'Mr Rimmer's dog ran on it
Last Christmas Eve
And there was nowt to bury.'

She's full of tales like these:
The woman who swallowed a python's egg;
The whale that was thrown up on the beach
With a Ford van in its stomach
And the driver still alive;
The man who cleaned the chimney
And his wife came back
And lit a fire.

We watch a sparrow settle
On the length of steel.
He hops and sings to us
While the murderous voltage
Pours beneath his feet.
My dad has told me
All there is to know
Of electricity and death.
Sparrows are safe
As long as they're not earthed.
'Unless,' says Rosie,
'They have one leg
That's really long.'

We walk down Station Road,
Our four eyes skinned
For limping sparrows
With uneven legs.
It's for things like this,
I try to tell the gang,
I walk home
With Rosie McAluskey.

The Hedgehog

Look, here he comes a-visiting
My bristle brush, my mate
Up from the bottom privet hedge
To my breakfast plate.
Here he comes a-trundling
On his jacked-up legs
Past our Megan's washing
And the string bag full of pegs.
Eh, I'm glad to see thee, Mister
Good morning, how d'you do?
With your hunched back full of arrows
And your black nose wet with dew.
Don't need no invitation
To pleasure my old eye
Come up and see me any time
My hedgerow Samurai.

A Young Girl Came Riding

A young girl came riding
Through the mists of dawn
Where the moon's pale light
Cast a stream of white
Through the standing corn.

Her eyes they shone like amethyst
Her brow was ivory
Her yellow hair
In the dawn's sweet air
Streamed like the starlit sea.

Silent as dew to the meadow
Silent as light to the day
Silent as breath
In the mouth of death
She came where the sick girl lay.

She sang an ancient carol
Born in reverie
While her mare in the sedge
At the woodland edge
Cropped the grasses soundlessly.

One young girl came riding
Where night-time met the day
But by the gleam
Of the sun's first beam
Two girls rode away.

Badger

I caught last night in the headlight's beam
My neighbour Brock again
Rolling his raggedy backside
Ambling along the lane
Like some old and weary farmhand
Strolling homeward from the inn;
Never hurried in his life
Too old now to begin.
I imagined him crossing his threshold
Turning the key in the lock
Settling down by the fireside
And grumbling to Mrs Brock:
'Who you reckon I seed just now
Roaring around the place?
Only that crack-brained wazzuck
One of they human race
A-driving his flash girt motor
Round the place again
Lights a-blazing, honking his horn
You'd think he owned our lane.'

Before the Beginning

Sometimes in dreams I imagine
Alone and unafraid
I'm standing in the darkness
When the first bright stars were made.

When the sun sprang out of the blackness
And lit the world's first dawn
When torrents of rock rained upwards
And the mountains and seas were born.

And I'm there when the forests and meadows
Flowered for the very first time
When eyeless legless creatures
Oozed upwards out of the slime.

But when I awake and read the books
Though they tell me more and more
The one thing they never tell me
Is – what was there before ...

Rubble

Pam found them;
Five small kittens
Huddled, fumbling, blind and wet
Beside the broken generator
In the crumbling outhouse
Pete and Frank were pulling down.
The mother didn't have a name.
'Must have wandered in
From one of the farms above the hill,'
My mother said
Tickling the tabby behind the ears.
'What d'you think this is, puss?
A maternity hospital?'

One by one we found
New homes for four of them.
Even the tabby mother
Didn't come to her saucer one day
And that was the last we saw of her.
The boisterous ginger
We adopted by default
Since no one seemed to want him
Something in the glinting of his eye
Made prospective owners
Mumble some excuse
And walk away.

Rubble, we christened him
In honour of the place
Where he was born
And he was trouble from the start.
Pavarotti of the night
From early days
He fell in love with stars
And sang them endless, raucous arias
That would have jerked
The graveyard dead
To channering wakefulness.
Then with the dawn
He'd totter home
Weary, punch-drunk, scarred,
And flop upon the couch
Before the fire
Like some old bruiser
Waiting for the water
And the flapping towel.
Most days, by way of thanks
He'd drop a tiny corpse;
A mouse, a squirrel or a mole
Upon our slate doorstep
Then lick his folded paw
And preen himself
Lazily surveying his fiefdom

Like a battered warlord
Fresh returned from victory in the field.
Then later on as he grew older
He'd crawl upon your lap
Blink slow his yellow eyes
Purr like a dynamo in bliss
And let you with some grace
Scratch him beneath the chin
Just long enough to let you think,
– At last, the old warrior's
Settling down and growing soft
Before, when least expected,
He'd unsheath his needling claws
And sink them deep as agony
Into the softness of your flesh.
All this while flashing you
The beatific smile that said,
'You can't imagine
The pleasure I derive
From simply being
What I am.'

Basil

When Cousin Basil
Played his bassoon
His body blew up
Like a barrage balloon
When I asked him shouldn't
He suck not blow
He swiftly answered
NOOOOOOOOOOOOOOOOOOOOOOOOOOOOOOO
OOOOOOOOOOOOOOOOOOOOOOOOOOOOOOOO
OOOOOOOOOOOOOOOOOOOOOOOOOOOOOOOO
OOOOOOOOOOOOOOOOOOOOOOOOOOOOOOOO
OOOOOOOOOOOOOOOOOOOOOOOOOOOO
OOOOOOOOOOOOOO
OOOOOOO
OOOO
OO
O
O
O
O
O
O
O
O
O
O
O
O
O

Bedmobile

I hear my grandad on the stair
He's counting, One Two Three
Bringing a rosy apple plucked
From my special climbing tree.
He brings the garden in with him
The flowers and the air
And there are twigs and petals
Tangled in his hair.
And as I eat my apple
He sits down next to me
Turning an imaginary wheel.
'Where to today?' says he.
And we drive our deluxe Bedmobile
To school along the heath
With the apple dribbling sweetness
Clenched between my teeth.

A Poem For A Very Special Person.

Listen
Will you do something for me?
Will you?
I want you to read this poem
Silently, carefully
And don't look surprised
When you find out
Who it's about.
Are you ready with your
'I'm not surprised' look?
Wait for it
This poem is about ...
       YOU!
         YES YOU!
Well then, how does it feel
To have a poem written about you?
What d'you mean you don't like it?
Staring?
Of course they're all staring,
That's the whole point.
What's that?
You wish the poem had been about someone else?
I would have to pick on you, wouldn't I?
Look why not point back?

Make out it's one of them.
Go on. Point at somebody.
No, not him
Nobody would write a poem about him.

Or her
Or ...
Well, maybe.
It's not working?
They're still staring?
You're not enjoying this too much, are you?
You see
That's another thing I know about you
You're one of those people
Who doesn't like
Having poems written about them.
Hurt? Me, hurt?
Of course I'm not hurt.

Poets are used to that sort of thing.
Tell you what. Here's a thought.
Just quietly, secretly
Close the book and
Slip it into your desk.
Wait!
Better still
Just leave it lying about
In a public place.

Someone is bound to pick it up
And think the poem is about them.
People are like that.

Pearl

Pearl, Jemima
Alfreton-Hughes
Turned into a lightbulb
And blew her fuse
Out in the town
They noticed her plight
By the switch on her back
And her head burning bright
When she fell asleep
This light-hearted girl
Hung upside down
Like a fifty watt Pearl
'Please,' begged Pearl
With a nervous cough,
'Whatever you do
Don't switch me off.'

Eat It All Up

Skinny Denise looked at her tea
And wouldn't touch a thing
Said her mother, 'My dear, you're not going out
Till you've eaten up everything.'

'Everything, Mother?' said Skinny Denise
Shuffling in her seat
Then she picked up her knife and fork and began
To eat and eat and eat.

She drenched the cod in strawberry jam
While her mother watched in a daze
As her daughter washed three kippers down
With a gallon of mayonnaise.

'Manners, my dear!' her mother said,
But nothing could stop Denise
As she tore into fifteen Eccles cakes
Spaghetti and mushy peas.

Now all the food had disappeared
But she hadn't finished yet
She began to chew the tablecloth
The mat and the serviette.

Then she attacked the table
Without using knife or fork
Crunching the legs between her teeth
As if they were steaks of pork.

When the TV set went the way of the rest
Her parents stared in dismay
As a voice within Denise announced,
'Here is the News for Today.'

Next to go was the Afghan rug
The windows, the fireplace, the doors
The sofa, the chairs – they all disappeared
Into those cavernous jaws.

The floorboards made her lick her lips
The taste of the walls made her sigh
And when she'd eaten the ceiling and roof
For afters she ate the sky.

Her mother sat in the ruins and asked,
'What was all that about?'
'I ate it all up,' said Skinny Denise,
'So now may I please go out?'

There and Back Again

Benny went ballooning
Across the countryside
Beyond the cliffs of Dover
Across the oceans wide.
He took with him his lurcher dog
And some mincemeat for his tea
And a change of clothes for Sunday best

And a Chinese dictionary.
The sun shone down on Benny
It shone down on the Earth
It glistened on the dolphins
Who leapt amd smiled with mirth.
And Benny saw a million sights
No man had seen before
So he flew across to Africa
And saw ten million more.
Then as he flew back home, he thought,
How famous I will be.
But his mother shouted, 'Wash your hands
Before you have your tea.'

Turkey and Pig

Said the Turkey to the Pig
With his feathers all awry.
'We must dance a flaunty jig
Before we have to fly.
With my clogs upon my feet
Let us dance into the blue.'
And the Pig he snorted, **'Oink oink.'**
And the Turkey said, **'Gobble gobble goo.'**

Said the Pig unto the Turkey,
'Oh, tell me, where are you?
The weather's turned quite murky
And the fog's like Irish Stew.
The débutantes are smirking
The orchestra's on cue.'
And the Pig snorted, **'Oink oink'**
And the Turkey said, **'Gobble gobble goo.'**

Said the Turkey to the Pig,
'Have you noticed my new dress?
I ran it up this morning
Out of dill and watercress
I shall flirt with yon euphonium
Tell me his name dear, do.'
Said the Pig, **'I think it's Oink Oink
Or possibly Gobble Gobble Goo.'**

'My joy is semolina,'
Ran Pig's jocular refrain.
'One can get it from the Queena
One can get it on the brain.
If the orchestra would play it
To an air I heard in Crewe
I'll do the honours on the **oink oink**
If you'll sing **gobble gobble goo.**'

Quoth the Turkey quite infuriate,
'You are stepping on my clothes
And there's a dwarfish curiate
Who is peering up my nose.
Oh, Piglet, I'm convulsed with shame
Whatever shall I do?'
And the Pig said, **'You try oink oink
And I'll try gobble gobble goo.'**

'We're caviar to the general
And leek soup to the rest
We have raced with fourteen tandems
And shown them who is best.
We have marched on whelks through Asia
And loved in Kathmandoooooooooooo
Oh, the world has heard our **oink oink**
And our **gobble gobble gobble gobble goo.'**

So that is where we leave them
On the uncharted shores of Time
Knowing naught can ever grieve them
While they're running through this rhyme
For they're dancing down a road of dreams
Hand in hand into the blue
And the shadows echo back their song,
Oink oink and ***gobble gobble goo.***

Scatterbrain

Before he goes to bed at night
Scatterbrained Uncle Pat
Gives the clock a saucer of milk
And winds up the tabby cat.

Young Lions Poetry Books

The Song that Sings the Bird
Ruth Craft

Salford Road and Other Poems
Gareth Owen

Song of the City
Gareth Owen

Toughie Toffee
ed. David Orme

Hairy Tales and Nursery Crimes
Michael Rosen

A Children's Zoo
ed. Julia Watson

The Lions Book of Young Verse
ed. Julia Watson

Rabbiting On
Kit Wright

All at £2.99

The Littles by John Peterson
£2.50

The Littles are tiny people who live in the walls of Mr Bigg's house. They eat whatever the Biggs eat, and help them out when they can. Trouble starts when the Biggs go on holiday and the Littles are threatened by an invasion of mice. Desperate measures are needed!

The Littles to the Rescue by John Peterson
£2.50

The dangerous Ground Tinies have captured Aunt Lily Little, who is on an errand of mercy to Mrs Little. Will, Tom and Dinky Little set off to rescue her.

Tom Little's Great Hallowe'en Scare
by John Peterson
£2.25

Uncle Nick comes to live with the Little family, and Tom plays a joke on his parents. It goes wrong, and the whole family is thrown into terrible danger.

The Littles Take a Trip by John Peterson
£2.50

Tom and Lucy Little are delighted when Cousin Dinky organises a meeting of all the tiny families close by. The journey there is more difficult than they'd anticipated, and the Littles get into fearful danger. Tom goes for help, but it is Lucy Little who saves the day.

Dr Jekyll and Mr Hollins by Willis Hall
£2.75

Nothing ordinary happens when the Hollins family go on holiday, and their trip to London is no exception – Henry's father swallows the wrong medicine by mistake and is unexpectedly turned into a hideous monster! Poor Henry tries desperately to get him changed back before he causes too much trouble!

The Mona Lisa Mystery by Pat Hutchins
£2.75

No one suspects what is in store for Class 3 of Hampstead Primary School when they board the school bus for their trip to Paris. The children are soon entangled with a group of art thieves intent upon stealing the Mona Lisa.

The Curse of the Egyptian Mummy
by Pat Hutchins
£2.75

As the bus carrying the 15th Hampstead Cub Scouts nears their campsite there is a radio news flash: an unidentified body, the victim of a deadly snake bite, has been found in the village. Then strange things start to happen. Is the curse of the Egyptian Mummy at work?

Josie Smith by Magdalen Nabb

Josie Smith lives with her mum in an industrial town; she is a resourceful, independent little girl who always does what she thinks best, but often lands herself in trouble.

Josie Smith at the Seaside by Magdalen Nabb

Josie Smith makes friends with a girl called Rosie Margaret; with the donkey, Susie; and with a big friendly dog called Jimmie, who swims off with Josie Smith's new bucket.

Josie Smith at School by Magdalen Nabb

More muddles and misunderstandings for Josie Smith. She is horribly late for lessons when she tries to get a present for her new teacher. And then she helps her new friend to write a story and completely forgets to do her own homework!

Josie Smith and Eileen by Magdalen Nabb

Josie Smith doesn't always like Eileen because Eileen has things that Josie Smith longs for – a birthday party, a bride doll, and the chance to be a bridesmaid in a long shiny pink frock. But Josie is happy in the end.

You can see Josie Smith in the Granada TV serial, *Josie Smith*.

All at £2.75

Lucy and the Big Bad Wolf
by Ann Jungman

When Lucy Jones goes to visit her grandparents wearing her new red anorak, she has no idea she will meet the Big Bad Wolf. The wolf follows her to London, where he soon finds himself thoroughly out of his depth – and Lucy finds herself involved in lots of amazing adventures.

Lucy and the Wolf in Sheep's Clothing
by Ann Jungman

The wolf returns to London to look up his old friends, and rapidly becomes the most wanted wolf in the city. As the police search for him, he tries to find a foolproof disguise, with hilarious results. And when a businessman called Sir Samuel Wolf is kidnapped – well, we can all guess who's behind it!

Lucy Keeps the Wolf from the Door
by Ann Jungman

When the wolf becomes the proud father of three little wolf cubs, things change: the granny-muncher of the fairy tale is gone, replaced by a vegetarian campaigner against acid rain. But *some* things never change, and the wolf's talent for causing chaos is one of them...

All at £2.99

My Best Fiend by Sheila Lavelle
£2.99

Angela's ideas frequently lead to disaster, and somehow it's usually
Charlie who takes the blame – and whose idea was it to set Charlie's
dad's garage on fire so he could rebuild it with the insurance money?
No prizes for guessing!

Disaster with the Fiend by Sheila Lavelle
£2.99

"Sabotage!" said Angela. "That's how we'll fix the cookery contest!
We'll put something really nasty in Delilah's cake!" As usual,
Angela's plan means that Charlie gets into trouble, but this time
nothing turns out quite as she'd intended.

Holiday with the Fiend by Sheila Lavelle
£2.99

Charlie would rather have gone on holiday with a killer whale than
Angela Mitchell, even though she promises not to get Charlie into
any trouble. Things get off to a bad start when Angela dyes
Charlie's hair...with disastrous results!

Trouble with the Fiend by Sheila Lavelle
£2.99

Angela Mitchell is back again with some new and hair-raising ideas –
like buying a wine-making kit as a present for Charlie's dad. Then
the trouble starts: neither knows how yeast works, and disaster
looms in the air...

The Demon Bike Rider by Robert Leeson
£2.25

There was a ghost on Barker's Bonk: a horned demon that made a terrible howling noise as it glided along in the dusk – on a bicycle. Mike and friends thought the bike-riding ghost could only be a joke until they saw and heard it; then suddenly they were running so fast there was no time to laugh.

Challenge in the Dark by Robert Leeson
£2.50

His first week at the new school is a challenge for Mike Baxter – not least when he makes an enemy of Steven Taylor and his bullying older brother, Spotty Sam. But the dare that both accept, of staying in the cold, dark silence of a disused underground shelter, leads to an unexpected friendship.

Wheel of Danger by Robert Leeson
£2.25

When Mike and his friends discover a disused mill out on the moors, it offers an exciting challenge: to get the water wheel working again. But the summer holiday adventure turns to danger when the mill race floods – and three of the children are trapped in the wheel house, with the water rising fast...

Fearless Fiona and the Mothproof Hall Mystery by Karen Wallace
£2.75

When Fearless Fiona gets a call on her mobile phone, she knows her dad's newspaper is in trouble. She needs a story – fast! Then she remembers Mothproof Hall. Solve the mystery of the priceless stolen rubies, and the paper will be saved!

All About Sam by Lois Lowry
£2.99

Being Anastasia Krupnik's younger brother isn't easy, but Sam gets by. There are other things that are worse, like broccoli, and not being able to have a pet because Dad's allergic to fur – until Sam finds a *bald* pet...

Carrot Top by Nigel Gray
£2.99

Carrot Top! That's what all the kids call Melinda, a little girl with a bright personality and bright red hair to match. And whether it's helping Dad with the wallpapering, playing with her friends or celebrating her birthday, every day is a new adventure.

Speedy Fred by Josephine Haworth
£2.99

Fred doesn't like staying with his grandfather in the country, and he's terrified of Uncle Joe's horse, Black Bob. And when Grandad's bike runs out of petrol and they're stuck on the moor, guess who has to ride and get help?

Order Form

To order direct from the publishers, just make a list of the titles you want and fill in the form below:

Name ....

Address ....

....

....

Send to: Dept 6, HarperCollins Publishers Ltd, Westerhill Road, Bishopbriggs, Glasgow G64 2QT.

Please enclose a cheque or postal order to the value of the cover price, plus:

UK & BFPO: Add £1.00 for the first book, and 25p per copy for each addition book ordered.

Overseas and Eire: Add £2.95 service charge. Books will be sent by surface mail but quotes for airmail despatch will be given on request.

A 24-hour telephone ordering service is avail-able to Visa and Access card holders: 041-772 2281